Zadie
and the Stripey Sock

Barbara Nye

penny
candy
BOOKS

Penny Candy Books
Oklahoma City & Greensboro

 This book is printed on paper certified to the environmental and social standards of the Forest Stewardship Council™ (FSC®).

Photo credit: Christopher Irons
Design: Shanna Compton
Special thanks to Christopher, Grace, Hillary, and Woodley for their enthusiastic support and objective early readings.

Small press. Big conversations.
www.pennycandybooks.com

Library of Congress Cataloging-in-Publication Data

Names: Nye, Barbara, author, illustrator.
Title: Zadie and the stripey sock / Barbara Nye.
Description: Oklahoma City : Penny Candy Books, 2021. | Audience: Ages 4-8.
  | Audience: Grades K-1. | Summary: Tired of being ignored, Zady decides
  to run away, but as she packs she realizes one of her favorite stripey
  socks is missing and interrogates each member of her family to its
  whereabouts.
Identifiers: LCCN 2021018002 (print) | LCCN 2021018003 (ebook) | ISBN
  9781736031926 (hardcover) | ISBN 9781736031933 (epub) | ISBN
  9781736031933 (mobi) | ISBN 9781736031933 (pdf)
Subjects: CYAC: Lost and found possessions--Fiction. | Socks--Fiction. |
  Runaways--Fiction. | Family life--Fiction. | LCGFT: Picture books.
Classification: LCC PZ7.1.N935 Zad 2021 (print) | LCC PZ7.1.N935 (ebook)
  | DDC [E]--dc23
LC record available at https://lccn.loc.gov/2021018002
LC ebook record available at https://lccn.loc.gov/2021018003

25 24 23 22 21   1 2 3 4 5

This book is dedicated to my mother, Evelyn Green, who never stopped learning and knew that reading books opens and sharpens minds.

Zadie stormed into her room and slammed the door.
"Nobody in this family ever listens to me!"

She thought of all the fun jobs she could
do when she ran away from home.

"We'll take only the most important things," Zadie told Archibald the Bear. So she packed her diary, a piece of toast, her soccer trophy, and her snorkel.

She added her six favorite books. Then one more.
And a banana. And her binoculars.
But something was missing.

She couldn't run away without her rainbow
stripey socks! But there was only one stripey
sock in the drawer.

"I have two feet," Zadie told Archie.
"I need two stripey socks."

She looked everywhere.

The missing sock was not
in the bathtub, not under
the kitchen table . . .

not in the cat's basket.

"Where is my other stripey sock?" she asked Jack.
"Did you put it in the washer?"

Jack rolled his eyes. "Is this it?" he laughed.

"That's not funny," said Zadie.
She marched out.

"Maggie, where is my other stripey sock?
Did you make one of your dumb sculptures
with it?" she asked.

"Stripes are not cool," said Maggie.
"Yes they are!" said Zadie. Out she went.

Banjo was chewing something in the grass.

"Oh no!" cried Zadie.

But it was Jack's favorite T-shirt off the laundry line. It was covered in dog slobber.

Zadie breathed a sigh of relief.

"Dad, do you know where my other stripey sock is?" asked Zadie.

He shook his head. "Do you know where the lawnmower is?" he asked.

Zadie stamped off.

"Nobody in this family cares about me, Archie," she said.

"Mom, do you have my stripey sock?
I need it now. I'm running away!"
she said.

Mom kept looking at her phone.

"Are you sure about that? I think Jack's making spaghetti tonight. Zadie, I need to make a phone call. Can you play with Sollie for a little while?" Mom asked.

Zadie wanted to scream. But she couldn't. Mom was on the phone. She stomped on the carpet a few times. She threw a cushion on the floor. She felt a little better.

Then she heard Sollie laughing in the next room.

"Look Zadie! I found a rainbow snake," said Sollie. "His name is Bruce, and he lives behind the couch. Ssssss."

Zadie looked at the stripey sock in her hand.

She slowly pulled it on over her fingers,
over her wrist, over her elbow.

It *was* a perfect stripey rainbow snake.

"I found one too," said Zadie. "Look, Sollie, my rainbow snake is sad. She needs a friend."

"It's okay," said Sollie. "She can play with me."

Maybe tomorrow would be a better day to run away, thought Zadie.

Besides, it was spaghetti night.